The Creakling

Best Wishes!

The Creakling

a novella

Jason C. Dykehouse

Urlundi Publishing

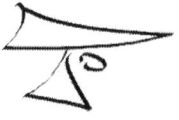

Copyright © 2024 Jason C. Dykehouse

All rights reserved

The characters and events portrayed in this book are fictitious. Any similarity to real persons, living or dead, is coincidental and not intended by the author.

No part of this work may be reproduced, or stored in a retrieval system, or transmitted in any form or by any means, electronic, mechanical, photocopying, recording, or otherwise, without express written permission of the publisher.

www.jasoncdykehouse.com

Printed in the United States of America

For David
For J. Arnold
For Friends

HOLDING HIS LUNCH PAIL by its rim, young Tommy Jones Calhoun strode homeward along the trace of a wagon trail. That morning, the handle of his pail had finally finished rusting off. When it did, the little bell pepper—but not the ash-roasted potato or the two raw carrots—fell to the ground. Tommy dusted off the pepper against his shirt before dropping it back into the pail and taking up his pace again toward school. Maybe three months earlier, the pail's cylindrical wooden grip had split away, leaving only the heavy-gauge handle wire for his fingers to hold. Still, the pail had worked just fine. Not much weight to carry, anyway. And today, the pail still worked just fine without any handle on it at all.

Every month or so, and usually on a Saturday, Tommy and Pawpa would hitch up the oxcart and ride into Little Lavaca, two miles away—for supplies and such, and for the county's weekly newspaper. It spoke of everything near and far and it even had a weekly joke that Pawpa got and Tommy sometimes did. And, it had the serious "Agriculture" page. But first, Pawpa would have his shave and his half-hour soak in the bathhouse. "My luxury," Pawpa would say. "Someday, Tommy, you'll have luxuries. And more of them. You'll see." Tommy's baths were at home. Two buckets of sulfury well water. Tommy always smelt of sulfur. Schoolkids said it often enough for it to be true. It's funny how you can't really smell your own self, but other people can smell you.

Whenever Pawpa was in the Little Lavaca bathhouse, Tommy stayed outside with the cart and Big Waddle and So-Soda. Oxen can stay still for hours. So could Tommy, who softly watched people passing by. Almost all of them had better clothes. And twice a year—on the two special Sundays—they'd also go into town. For service. "For the sake of Christ's holiness," Pawpa made clear. And Pawpa always made sure that they each had a new shirt for the springtime service. Of course, those shirts would be well worn or even worn out altogether by the time of winter service. But that's when Preacher Baxter would give Pawpa his spring dollar coins back. It happened twice. "Just what I tithed," Pawpa said. "Always give, Tommy," Pawpa said. "What you do always finds its way back."

But Pawpa didn't get any coins back this year, and he didn't mention it. But Tommy thought about it. The year was tough, what with the little drought and all. Preacher probably used Pawpa's money right, Tommy decided.

Once after the winter service, Tommy saw something glorious at the center of the cart seat as he stepped up on a wheel rung to get into the cart to head home. It was a boxed quarter of an apple pie. They smiled at each other as they ate their two, halved pieces at home together—after they secured the oxen and even washed their hands real good, because of how special that pie would be. They thought that cutting their pieces in half might save their other halves for tomorrow. But they were wrong. They finished one piece and then, with a flash of a look at each other, they dug into their seconds. Delicious. Tommy liked that memory of eating with Pawpa. So sweet. Cinnamony. Pawpa said the crust was flakey and that's how a pie's supposed to be. Tommy smiled and nodded quickly, licking sugary thickness from his lips.

But that pie appeared only once. And that was maybe five years ago, some months after everything happened. Tommy checked around the oxcart seat after the next winter service when Pawpa wasn't looking. He didn't want his grandfather to think he was disappointed if he was caught looking for nothing. And nothing was there. He didn't even look after the last two winter services, but he thought about it along those rides home. And now, the winter service was just over a month away. He wanted just one more piece of apple pie. Maybe just once a year. A luxury.

Whenever he headed on foot to or from town along the wagon trace, Tommy walked the right wheel track. He did so both toward town and back home again the other way. Always on the right side. Every school day he did that. For maybe two full years now. "Keepin' the trace. Keepin' it clear and even," he used to sing to himself repeatedly in a made-up singsong. He was deliberate about walking like that. He'd sometimes even dance in his stupid singsong. Walking the trace on the right side was a kind of discipline he carried out daily. And he partly knew why. Grasses and mesquite—and that new-sproutin' and spreadin' thorny huisache brush—had been encroaching upon the way. Plus, the cart rides were fewer now, and wagon rides were long gone with Pawpa's necessary selling of the horses. Three years, now? The horse wagon rested weather-worn back behind the barn. And Tommy didn't even play on it. Not anymore. Early on, in the months after things changed, he used to play on the wagon, pretending to be heading back east or something. But he'd been here all his life. No one he knew had ever up and gone "Back East" as people talked about. Mister Donovan went east, but that was for the war. And he came back. But Tommy knew some people had gone and stayed back east. But he wouldn't know where to go if he tried. His job was to keep a trace open. To keep in contact with the world—with Little Lavaca.

When Ma and Pa were still here, the wagon rides took place once or even thrice every week. Ma would have one of Mawma's old quilts doubled twice over on the wagon bed for little Tommy to be on when they went into town. Real early on, Mawma and Pawpa were on their own quilt in the back, too, Tommy remembered. But Pawpa was sometimes on the bench, driving the wagon. Tommy wasn't sure why Pa wasn't there sometimes. That's when Mawma would lean close to Tommy, telling him stories. Stories about Germany when she was very young. About her early days and the Republic of Texas that no one really experienced direct-like before it became a state. Texicans, Mexicans, and Americans were a blur to Tommy back then. She hated the evil Comanche and she said why without giving the details. But it was bad. You had to rightly fear the Comanche, Tommy knew. Run without stopping. But she liked the

Lipan. She had Lipan friends. One Lipan family came around once when Tommy was real young. It was Mawma's Lipan friend's sister she never met before. And her man and three kids. All the men went hunting and brought back a doe. The two Lipan boys taught Tommy how to climb a live oak, flat-footed against the bark. They were maybe seven and eight years old. Tommy was younger, maybe five. The girl was even younger, three or maybe four. She couldn't climb yet, but she laughed when Tommy worked the well bucket, bringing up water and pouring it out and doing it again for her. She was so excited about that well water, Tommy remembers. They all had a feast late in the day and the Lipan slept in the barn that night. They left on foot in the early morning. Mawma gave them a quilt.

Mawma was always full of stories, and her quilts made it easier to ride out the bumps along the wagon trail. Sometimes, Tommy kneeled on the folded-over quilt behind his mother, looking forward over her shoulder. Sometimes, he sat down behind her, the back of his head against her spine, looking at whatever they were drawing away from. At the start of wagon rides to town, Pa always took up his side—and then some—of the wagon seat. "Gotta steer them horses, woman!" he once said long ago with a backhand to her side. "Give me some damn room!" Ma always did after that. Mawma was dead then and Pawpa wasn't in the wagon that day. And Tommy never once sat leaning his head against Pa's spine after that. Ma's was better, and not only because she liked having him there.

Some school days, when Tommy felt enough strength or anger as he strode there or back again, he'd kick away new sprouts of huisache or fledgling grass clumps touching his path. Even so, every year brought more and more huisache—even during this year's little drought. Tough plants find ways to live, Tommy knew.

Some days, he wouldn't want to kill anything. He'd just walk the trace. And on the most recent of days, he had been setting his mind at least a little bit upon Loretta Mae Knapp, the girl from school he loved silently and with all his heart. He was so sure of that. She had three dresses. Plus that Sunday dress of hers. She had at least that

THE CREAKLING

one Sunday dress. Maybe she had more Sunday dresses. She was skinny, but not skinny like Tommy. Her teeth weren't that good. Tommy's were better. And she was eleven, too. He asked her age, once. At school. This very school year. That's all he ever said to her, asking her birth day after she moved into town. He didn't know why he even asked her that. He just did. He saw her looking at him once at recess a few weeks ago in October, maybe just a month after he talked to her. Another time, too, but he wasn't sure about that. He told Billy-Boy about her looking at him, and they decided she was pretty despite it all. Then she showed up several days ago at school on a Friday in her Sunday dress. "Just for fun," Loretta said to Miss Koehler when she commented on it. But just now, new huisache growth pricked at his pants, so he went back minding the trace and watching his step. Loretta would be there tomorrow. She was a good girl, and her attendance was good like Tommy's. He could hope for that. Pawpa almost always made him go to school. Tommy knew that Pawpa liked his "little quiet" each day alone on the farmstead. Tommy's schooling gave Pawpa that luxury at least. It provided Pawpa some peace. Tommy knew it was hard for Pawpa, too. Together, they were all they had left of before.

    Tommy was nearing home. The little stead was just around the low rise up ahead. He looked down to the mostly-eaten, ash-roasted potato in his pail. Just a chunk left. He had already picked off and eaten much of its skin. The remaining potato flesh was browned from exposure. Today, that was all that remained in his pail as he headed home. He smiled. "I do so love cooked potato skins," he said to himself.

    In recent months, Tommy almost never came home with nothing reserved from lunch. Worse than a just-filled stomach all through afternoon schooling was a grumbling, empty one upon reaching his home—especially if Pawpa should give him some straight-away choring. And supper was never waiting for them. Not anymore. Not since they died. So it was better to just make it home weakly in the late afternoon and still have something to bite into, chew, and swallow—maybe even two or three swallows. A chunk of potato. Better yet with skin. That was always better than making it home after a just-enough lunch with nothing left over. Tommy had learned that truth.

 He looked toward the live oak grove a long stone's throw from the barn, but something at the barn caught his eye. The window sash of the barn's tool room was hammered back into place. Old man that he was, Pawpa had been working, today. Tommy smiled.

 Tommy turned his look back toward the grove of six live oak trees and seven graves. His smile dropped slowly as he thought upon it all. Ma's two grandparents—Mawma's parents from her side—were there. They had tombstones. "That's called granite. It lasts forever," Pawpa said when Tommy asked as they were weeding again in the grove last year. They especially weeded around Ma's and Mawma's graves. Made them "about as nice as nice can be," Pawpa said when they were done. Tommy always thought that "granite" sounded right for his great-grans. He'd tell his own kids that when the time came to weed their own dead. Any of the dead, but especially those you really loved. He was sure of that. Because that's what Pawpa did. And Tommy was sure he'd do the same. Because everyone dies, and all you can do is get rid of the weeds.

 Mawma's brother and sister were in the grove, too. They had smaller granite stones. Tommy never knew them. They were dead. And the etchings of their names and dates weren't as deep as the great-grans' etchings. Less expensive tombstones. And Tommy couldn't think much at all on them. Something about the Atlantic. Holy Romans or something. Way back when. They died long ago on different years. Long dead before Tommy was around. His younger and dead baby sister that he couldn't remember ever seeing was there, too. But he thought about her. His sister. She had a rectangle slab of concrete Pawpa made special. It was a very small slab. Size of a pillow, Mawma said. Nothing else except an old, weathered, wooden cross. Pawpa and Ma replaced that wood cross with a new one once. No words were on it. His nameless sister. Tommy stood in the grove when they set about changing the cross. He was picking winter clover, looking for a lucky one.

Nowadays, Tommy sometimes stood in the grove alone. Looking at the graves and thinking over it all as he could. He remembered Ma being pregnant. Ma was screaming late one night, and Pawpa put him in the root pit. Told him to stay. It was dark cold in the pit. Ma was in Mawma's and Pawpa's bedroom bed for days after that, Tommy remembers. She was so weak, but she smiled at little Tommy and reached for his hand when he first saw her again. But there was no baby. That happens sometimes. Tommy even heard of that since then a couple of times from others. He figured out that babies don't make it. Sometimes mamas don't either. Teacher even said so afterward. And Ma had it real bad that night. He was put in the pit another time, too. But that time Ma didn't make it.

But he just couldn't remember Ma or Pa actually dying. But they did die. They must have. They were gone. And when Tommy left the pit a long, long time after he'd been put down into it, his Ma's grave was there. So she must have died. She was under a heap of stones. A big, flattish stone of some kind was set up as her tombstone. No marks. "Your Ma's grave," Pawpa said maybe that same day. But Pa wasn't there. "Buried away," Pawpa said. "He always wanted his own place, and he has it, now. Buried away." Tommy thought that sounded somehow right. Only sometimes when he was in the grove would he want to see a grave for Pa. Maybe near Ma's grave. But he always shook that thought off. It was best he wasn't close to her. Thinking on it all troubled him, so he tried not to think on it all.

Mawma was dead and buried in the grove, too. Pawpa found her dead behind the house. Sudden stroke or something. Five-year-old Tommy was carried in Ma's arms for maybe the last time when he saw his Mawma dead. Pa and Pawpa were closing up her coffin. Preacher Baxter and some others were there. Pa and Pawpa had dug her grave pit. Later they and some other men lowered her into it. Preacher said some things and then it all ended with a piling of dirt over her. But Mawma's burial place ended up being something special. Pawpa worked more days than one levelling the earth over her and then staking a rectangle of long lumber boards into place. He worked slow, patient-like. He then mixed and poured concrete over her. "A perfect slab," Pa said.

Little Tommy was in town with his parents and Pawpa when he learned that an obelisk Pawpa ordered all the way from New Orleans had arrived. That's when he finally understood what that word "obelisk" meant. They had all been talking about it for some time. It sounded mysterious.

Tommy was waiting on the quilt, looking at its patterns and following stitches when the rest of his family came out of the Little Lavaca Livery. Pa and Pawpa dropped the wagon tailgate, and Ma had Tommy move out of the way when she got up on the wagon bed. She spread Mawma's quilt out as four livery men trudged out with the obelisk boxed in lumber. They had to work hard getting it up onto the wagon bed. "Third time's the charm!" one said. Tommy remembered that saying. He had heard it before. Pa and Pawpa and Ma helped ease it down onto the bed. "Watch your fingers, Daddy," Ma said. "I know it," Pawpa said. Tommy remembered all of that.

Later, in the grove, Pa and Pawpa and Ma lowered the obelisk from the backed-up wagon onto Mawma's slab. Little Tommy even helped, looking at and watching for what he was told to look at and watch for. He didn't know what he was doing, but he remembered doing something. He knew he should be helpful. On the slab, the obelisk's lumber casing was easy to remove with Pawpa's iron bar and strong hands. Pa and Ma and Tommy picked up lumber pieces and put them into the wagon bed. Some are still saved in the barn's tool room. Ma showed Tommy how to set the lumber down soft-like, not just toss them in. Pa had already tossed a piece onto the wagon bed. It was all somehow real special, that day, so Tommy was given the job of putting the rest of the lumber in soft-like. Tommy thought Mawma would like it that he did that work soft-like.

Then it happened, something so strong from Pawpa. Even Pa said so. Pawpa held tight to the exposed obelisk and waddled it all by himself into place at the head of the slab. He rocked it forward one side at a time. It took some time, getting it there into place all alone. He'd move it some and then rest a moment before going back at it. Moving it into place. "It's almost as tall as Mawma was," Ma said in Tommy's ear. "And he's walkin' it into place." His ma was crying all silent. Tommy didn't know what to do, so he just stayed still, watchin' Pawpa rock that thing forward one corner and then the other. "Walking it" clear across Mawma's slab-topped grave. Like a moving hug. It's still there. "Walking" something is sometimes all you can do with things too heavy to bear.

Mawma's obelisk has a metal plaque on its slanted base with her name and dates and everything: "BELOVED SUNSHINE" is engraved below "Erna Heinrich Jones" and above "1810-1861" followed by a star. It was all real important to Pawpa. And he would sometimes sit on the slab when Ma and Pa were still alive. One day, from a distance, Tommy saw Pawpa's tall frame against the obelisk. He was holding it hard again, with his arms wrapped around it. And Pawpa was shaking or something and he made some loud noise. Little Tommy thought he was trying to move it again, but he wasn't. Ma turned Tommy around by his shoulders and sent him quickly inside the family's three-room, single-loft home. She stooped down and held his cheeks in her cupped hands and told him, "Don't you ever talk about this with Pawpa, Tommy Jones. Because that's how Pawpa loves you and how he loves me. His heart is bigger than both his big hands clutched together. He has us inside them, Tommy, but he doesn't have Mawma no more." Tommy understood.

Now, as Tommy strode alongside the length of the yellowing, five-foot-tall cornstalks of the two-acre cornfield, he remembered wanting—back on that day—to ask Ma if Pawpa also loved Pa that same way. He didn't ask. Maybe Preacher Baxter loved him that way. Supposed to love everybody. So maybe someone did. But Tommy didn't. And now it was another bad year for corn. He slowed a moment and smiled as he chose to think on Miss Knapp. Maybe she'd live here one day. This time it would be a lady moving in to the old Heinrich farmstead. Not Pawpa moving in with Mawma's family, and not later when Pa moved in with Ma and the family. She'd be "My Little Miss Knapp." He had been calling her that, if only to himself. That was his sweet thought as the weathered three-room home with a tall loft came into view. Weeds were thick on the cornfield side of the house and behind it. Maybe today he and Pawpa would take the weed whips to some of it before having something to eat. Weeks ago, Pawpa mentioned that they needed to do that. But that was a lot of weeding put off for too long, and the coming winter would kill off much of it anyway. Maybe that's why Pawpa didn't mention it again. Maybe he was just letting it grow. So Tommy smiled and looked at the closed shutters of the loft window on the other side of the house. He wondered if Loretta'd ever be up there with him some future year. And that thought got him somehow all flustered.

* * *

Inside, Pawpa was bootless and asleep, reclined on the old couch along the wall opposite the loft and near the woodburning stove at the transition from sitting room to kitchen area. A whisp of smoke visible beyond the ajar iron stove door meant the coals still had life. Pawpa could tend things just fine on the farm. He roused when Tommy closed the door.

"Aw, Tommy. I done slept the afternoon away, again."

"Yes, Pawpa."

There was a terse exhale and some little body creaks as Pawpa brought himself into a sit and then reached for his boots. "But I did a couple things and fixed that barn sash this morning, like we meant."

"I saw that, Pawpa." Tommy watched Pawpa flex a leg and then point its socked foot so as to put on one of his well-worn boots. Socks in need of darning. Pawpa was older than his age of maybe sixty. Doctor said he had the arthritis bad. And all the hard outside work weathered him some. "Any chores, Pawpa? Maybe we can well-water our good row of corn again."

THE CREAKLING

"Naw, Tommy. Maybe tomorra." He pressed off his knees and stood. "Plus, I birdshot us a few quail, today. Just before I set into my afternoon rest. I cut their heads off and drained 'em. They're on the table in that newsprint wrap. Pluck 'em and wash 'em off, but first get a big potato or two little ones and two carrots and an onion from the pit. Bring another pail of water, too. I'll get the stove goin' good and then cook us up our quail dinner."

Tommy looked at Mawma's rack of porcelain spice jars upon the kitchen wall above the prep table. He knew some of the jars didn't hold any spice anymore, and two of the jars were missing. When he was five, Tommy broke one of them when he knocked it off the table. Mawma held little Tommy to her side and told him that he had to be careful with precious things. She told him that she wouldn't tell Pa. If it came up, she'd say it fell while she was cooking. Tommy never heard it come up. Mawma liked her porcelain jar spice rack. Maybe it was one of her luxuries. She would keep them jars dusted off. Clean porcelain is glossy white. The jars were the brightest things in the house. Most were dusty, now.

On that day, little Tommy helped Mawma sweep up the shattered porcelain and wasted spice. It was nutmeg, he remembered. Maybe the apple pie had nutmeg. He remembered the smell. Mawma and Tommy took turns with the broom and dustpan cleaning it up. He remembered that time whenever he looked at the empty spaces in the spice rack. But today, he also smiled. Because Pawpa could spice up meat real good. Beef, wild game, fish from the pond way upstream, or poultry. Tommy missed having meat often. Pawpa cooked it good, too. Learned it from Mawma and her own Ma. Sometimes he'd buy spice in town and carefully refill up a jar or two when they got home. Sometimes he even brought greens from the field. "Good herbs," he'd say. And he liked cooking over mesquite the best. Tommy looked at the wrapped quail on the prep table. He couldn't remember Pa ever cooking.

Seeing Pawpa looking at him, Tommy started. "Oh, yes, Pawpa! I'd love me some quail." And with that, he headed back outside to the root pit in the knoll behind the house. He had a fine smile upon his face. Tonight, with the cornmeal flatbread, he would have more than enough in his belly. And another flatbread was always skilleted at suppertime for Tommy's breakfast. Pawpa made sure of that. Sometimes, they'd even each have two flatbreads in the morning. Sometimes even with fixins if the cart ride to town brought back a few eggs and maybe, just maybe, some bacon. But often it was only the flatbread with a shared chopped pepper and onion for breakfast. On some of those mornings, Pawpa would stovetop the chopped onion and pepper and add some salt and a touch of oil. They'd roll it all up into their flatbreads. Delicious. Pawpa tried so hard to make up for lost Ma and Mawma. And today, he even got some quail.

Ma once said that there weren't many root pits in South Texas and that Pawpa brought his idea with him from up north. He had to dig it extra deep this far south. And it was deep. Pawpa was an older young man and new to the family when he dug it. Took a long, long time, they all said. Almost a year, maybe. And it was still here. Mawma said Pawpa always worked so hard. She said it would be good if Tommy took after him. Tommy wanted to.

Back when Tommy played atop the knoll, it was like he had the shortest goldmine ever dug right down below him. With a long stick as a sword, he'd fight off pirates, Spanish-led Mexicans, Comanches, and even a bad Apache or federal or two if he had to. But his gold below shone like the sun. He worked hard for it. He treasured it. That was back when he would play.

In the building of the pit's depth, Pawpa heaved and sledged into place three sets of stout timber support beams that held up the six feet of earth above the pit. From the opening at the side of the knoll was a stepped slant of some ten feet into the narrow, eight-foot long pit lined on either side with shelving, which was now beginning to weaken from seasonal dampness and time. The steps, too, were failing, so you had to be careful. Two years ago or so, Pawpa said he should replace the wood steps with stone. Tommy used to be scared when he was sent down to get preserves or vegetables or what have

THE CREAKLING

you, but he knew now that only worms and insects and larva could be in the pit if the trap door stayed closed. And it was nearly pitch-black with the door closed. Pawpa sealed it good and kept it that way. You had to keep the vermin out.

Tommy didn't like the two times Pawpa closed the pit's trap door over him. But Pawpa said that it would be fine, and that he'd be back for Tommy soon. But it was a long time—two long times ago—that it happened. And Pawpa did come back, opening the door with one hand when he did. So easy. So strong. He was tall and strong. But Tommy remembers him quivering up there at the end of the slanted steps. Silent, too. Quivering like he was against the obelisk as he let Tommy out of the pit. Maybe that's not how it was. Maybe it was only the first time that he was quivering. It was two times, long ago.

You could never really play in the pit, because you must always close the trap door right away, lest the heat get in there for good. And that wouldn't be good. Plus, it was so dark in there with the trap door closed. And you'd be left alone. So the root pit wasn't for play. You'd just go in and get what you went getting after and then get out and close that trap door good. But winters were different. Because the air was cold. And it was nearly winter. But who plays outside when they're cold? Tommy didn't. He was skinny.

Today, Tommy walked briskly around the back of the house, which was mostly overtaken with weeds and grasses except for a footpath toward the little knoll just northeast of an old oak tree. That's where the pit was. Mostly shaded. He remembered seeing Pawpa and Mawma both coming out from there one day. They were already old like fifty-something, but they had happy faces. Pawpa was pushing her bottom up the rest of the narrow steps with one strong hand and holding the door open with the other. "Just taking stock on what I've got, Tommy," Pawpa said as he closed the door. "Good enough for any winter." Mawma thought that was funny, but she was looking away. She was straightening her dress. Nowadays, Tommy has another idea about what all that meant. But he wasn't sure. It was a long time ago.

It was always hard for Tommy to pull open the wide, short root pit trap door. He'd been ouched more than once working it open or closed, but he had learned to leverage it open and then set it down on his bent knee before shifting his grip and setting it down or lifting it up all the way as needed. "You have to be patient." That's the country rule.

So, Tommy went down into the pit again. He looked over the sad potatoes and then picked out two medium-small ones. He took two almost-limp carrots and a soft onion. They were all like that. They'd be far worse come January. But everything cooks soft anyways. He looked once again at the last jar of preserved peaches Mawma must have made all those years back. All by itself on a top shelf. The peaches looked like they might have turned bad. And Pawpa never asked for them all these last few years. And Tommy didn't ask Pawpa about it, because Pawpa had been down here enough all this time to know. Pawpa knew everything. Tommy wished he did, too.

* * *

That evening, as Tommy was drifting asleep in the rocking chair that Pawpa made for Ma, he licked up a grain of salt found just off his lips. His soft smile grew a bit larger as he took it in and swallowed. Quail makes for moist meat that can drip from your mouth, and Pawpa cooked it real smokey. And the carrots and the onion were fall-apart soft. Seasoned. Cinnamon carrots. Just a little sulfury. Just a little. Because of Pawpa. He seasoned things. And they even ate the meal off Mawma's mother's old Germany plates. It had been a long while since Pawpa brought them out. Precious. And the plates were full of food, but they both stayed careful with their forks and knives, because the plates were precious. With his eyes yet closed, Tommy Jones shifted in the rocker, thinking back on all of that as he drifted.

"I see your mother's face in yours when you're in that rocker," Pawpa said just loud enough for Tommy to rouse from his slumbering and look at Pawpa seated on the couch all the way on its left side as he'd do when Mawma was still here. She'd sit all up next to him after evening supper and other work. She'd be at his right shoulder. He'd hold her some. She and Ma would then quilt or darn or sew. They'd all talk. And that's when Pa would usually take his evening walk.

"How did they die, Pawpa? I just can't remember."

Pawpa shifted just a bit and tightened his lips after the question. He looked away to the window, even though the sun had been down for almost an hour. There was nothing but darkness beyond the window pane. "I told you, Tommy."

"Please, Pawpa. Tell me again," Tommy said softly, looking out the window, too. "I just can't remember any of it."

Pawpa's old body creaked a bit as he pushed off his knees and stood. He straightened upright and then, with a glance to Tommy, walked to the window. He exhaled slowly. Paused.

Tommy bit his lip a moment. "Was it bad, Pawpa? Is that when you put me in the pit the second time? Is that why I don't know anything? You can tell me if it was bad—even for Ma. I'm big enough, now. Was it bad for her like before when my baby sister died?"

Pawpa clenched his fists just slightly before relaxing them. He then set his forehead against the only pane of glass in the house. He shook his head slowly against it, squeaking the glass. Pawpa stopped. He straightened up again, looking at the unseeable in the darkness out the window. "It was that sickness that came around some years back, remember, Tommy? That Quick Fever, as some people called it. I don't know what science calls it. When it struck, it struck only here that time—not in town. And that's good. We stopped it from spreading, Tomas. It was the Quick Fever."

"How come I didn't see them sick?"

Pawpa breathed in and out slowly, still staring away. "It was Quick Fever. Quick Fever—or whatever they call it. You have to stay away from it." He turned to Tommy, who was making little rocking chair rocks off his toes. "You *had* to stop that fever,

Tommy. *Had to.* And we stopped it right here, Tommy. You and I. Your Pa was the last one. Remember? Even Sheriff Cartwright said we did right when I went into town after."

"Was I still in the pit when you talked to the sheriff?"

Pawpa paused only a second. "Yes, Tommy. You were in there a long time. A very long time. Until after the sheriff and I came back and buried your Ma and Pa. It was best that way. Kept you safe from all that sickness." He paused only a moment. "You go on to your loft, now."

Tommy stopped rocking. He looked at the floorboards a moment. "Yes, Pawpa."

Climbing the ladder to the loft, Tommy asked without looking back, "Are you going to sleep, Pawpa?"

"Naw. I think I'll walk the stead some."

Nearing the top of the loft, Tommy turned his look down to his grandfather on his mother's side. "Pawpa, you never sleep well at night when you rest all afternoon. Maybe you stay up too late."

Pawpa was heading to the door and turning his head toward Tommy without looking at him. "I know it, Tommy." He smiled. "But I just can't help but think over it all."

And with that, Pawpa went out to the darkness. Maybe to the grove. Maybe somewhere else. Walking after the sun was down. Just like Pa did, but not like Pa at all.

* * *

Tommy Jones Calhoun liked sleeping in the loft in Novembers. It was rarely too very cold up there, what with the glued newsprint sealing all the seams along the walls. "The poor man's wallpaper," Pa said. For the last couple of winters, during the cold nights that often came in December and January and sometimes February, he missed his Ma so much and sometimes even his Pa so much. Those were the months that the loft got cold, even with Pawpa tending the woodstove twice a night or more. But Pa was good for keeping him and Ma warm. They'd be happy then—Ma and Pa and Tommy—

THE CREAKLING

when it was cold and they were asleep together. Tommy liked that. But tonight, he was nestled on the old, wide mattress they slept upon in years past. He had one each of Mawma's and Ma's quilts over him and another of Mawma's real old ones folded up near one end of the sideboard if he needed it against the cold. His loft quilts used to smell like Ma and Pa. But not anymore. He used to cry silent a lot in the quilts after it all happened. And he'd be able to smell them. But not anymore. It even used to be easy to remember their smells. But not anymore. Last summer, he could just barely smell them in the quilts on the hottest nights. Maybe he would smell them next summer, too. But it was mid-November, 1867, and summer was a long way off. Last week, the fact that summer was so long off almost made him cry again.

But tonight, Tommy was fast asleep, curled up on the side of the mattress nearest the closed wooden loft window. If the place ever caught fire, Tommy knew he would have to drop down out of the loft to the ground even though it would hurt something fierce. Pa taught him that. That it would hurt. Maybe break a leg or worse. But Pa said Tommy would have to just drag himself away from the burning house if he and Ma and the rest didn't make it out. Drag himself to the well. Just drag himself through the pain. Someone would see the glow or smoke of the fire and come to save him. Pa could be real serious sometimes. Even Pawpa nodded when Pa told Tommy this.

And then, just now, something from outside hit the closed shutters of the loft window. Waking from deep sleep, Tommy opened his eyes in the darkness.

"Tommy Jones!" Pawpa called from outside. "Open that loft window!"

Drowsily, Tommy flopped over toward the window as he threw off the quilts from his upper body. In his twisting, the quilts became wrapped around his legs slowing him as he dragged himself an extra pull to the window. Kneeling up to it, he unlatched it's two-foot by two-foot door and pushed it open. He was half-asleep with his head half-way out of the loft, fifteen feet above the ground. In the light of the waning gibbous Moon, he saw Pawpa down below and he tensed. He was still trapped in the quilts. "Is it a fire, Pawpa!" he cried out as he tried to kick his legs free from the quilts. He was afraid. "Pawpa! I'm trapped!"

Pawpa was smiling and reaching up. "It's all right, Tommy," he said soft-like. A falling star zipped in the sky above and behind Pawpa. Then another one did.

"I just saw two fallin' stars, Pawpa."

"I know it! Look up. Look up at Leo like I taught you." He was pointing.

Another falling star went by. Tommy widened his eyes and looked up and found the Big Dipper near Pawpa's point. He then followed his imagined line from the Dipper's front two stars down to Leo. That's where they were coming from. Another falling star and then two almost at the same time. And then another. "Pawpa!"

"It's a shower, Tommy. Come on outside with me."

But Tommy kept looking into the sky, turning his look at each new falling star. "The sky's full of them, Pawpa!"

"I know it, Tommy. Come down."

Tommy untwisted the quilts from his legs and then eased his feet down onto the affixed loft ladder reaching down to the sitting room. Moonlight showed the way to the open door and outside. Pawpa was looking up with his hands on his hips. His jaw was slack and the Moon shone in his eyes. He was smiling a smile Tommy didn't know if he'd ever seen on Pawpa's aging face. But there was something familiar about it. Maybe from before it all happened. Maybe back when Tommy was real young and Mawma was still alive. It was a nice smile for Pawpa. Tommy watched it rather than the falling stars as he walked up. Shoeless and shirtless, Tommy held himself against the light chill.

"Tommy, this is what they call a meteor shower. I don't know if the paper will call it a storm, but it's faintly like the one I'm sure I told you about more than once. And it's out of Leo again."

"I remember. It kinda lit up the night, you and Mawma said. A hundred every second."

"At least."

"Oh look at that one!" Tommy called out, pointing to a large, fragmenting one. "It had colors!"

Pawpa nodded. Tommy could see that Pawpa was happy. And that made Tommy happy. "Tell me again about the storm."

Pawpa looked toward the grove for a moment, nodding. The granite tombstones were almost glowing—what with the moonlight through the gaps in the leaves. They always glowed in the moonlight. The cement burial works that Pawpa set didn't glow, but you could make them out. But you couldn't make out Tommy's sister's wooden cross that was there. Not bright enough. Pawpa cleared his throat. "Sunshine—*Mawma*—ran over to me after it started—woke me up from the window of the shed I was staying in. Almost four miles she ran. She said she wanted to make sure I'd see it. This was shortly after I moved down from Missourah Territory, working over at the Lindheimer farmstead. That was . . . thirty-three, thirty-four years ago?" He shook his head and went back to his slack-jawed smile for a long moment. "It was plum near four in the morning. It was magical, Tommy. That was when I asked Mawma to marry me. It was like my life finally began when she said yes and we held each other in a long, long embrace looking up together. The sky was full of falling stars, Tommy. A downpour. I looked at Sunshine, and she was brightened by the storm. I've never seen nothing more beautiful as her face on that night, looking up to the heavens." Pawpa suddenly cleared his throat. His eyes teared up. He snuffled in, shook his head, and wiped his face.

Tommy took and held that hand after Pawpa set it back on his hip. He held onto it tight even though Pawpa started to move it away at first. "She's like that apple pie, we had together. Remember, Pawpa?"

Pawpa looked down to Tommy, maybe ten inches shorter than he was. Maybe half his weight. "I can see your mother, Tommy Jones, and maybe even some of Mawma in ya." He welled again and wiped his face with his other hand. "I have no more words tonight, Tommy Jones."

"I know, Pawpa. And I just love you so much!" He hugged on tight to his grandfather. After standing still for maybe four seconds, Pawpa hugged some back. It was then that Tommy's eyes welled and shut closed. Two tears ran off his cheeks as another one—one from Pawpa—landed on his bare shoulders. There was hope. And for a moment, Tommy was happy again.

But then came the thud. A large, dull thud. Very close. And that's when Tommy Jones Calhoun and Samuel "Pawpa" Jones released their holds on each other and returned to being the men they were: men living far outside of town in the huisache and mesquite wilderness of South Texas. They looked around.

"From the cornfield." Tommy stated.

"That's what I thought."

"A mountain lion? A bear?" Tommy was staring, wide eyed into the rows of moonlit corn. "It was big."

"Don't know. It sounded like something hitting the earth, falling flat and hard."

"Best get your shotgun, I think, Pawpa."

"Yessir. And we best both get inside."

"Yessir." Tommy started moving, heading inside with Pawpa close behind him.

* * *

Tommy ended up sleeping on the old couch. He did that some nights over the last few years on warmer months when Pawpa would sleep in the bedroom with the window shutters open. Pawpa usually only slept on the couch at night when it was the colder months, so he could tend the fire. Plus, it was easier for him to "step outside and piss" once or twice or even sometimes thrice during the night. They had an old pot they used to keep just outside for that. But with only Tommy and Pawpa now, it was kept inside by the door. Pawpa emptied it in the outhouse every morning. "Men have to piss more as they age on up, Tommy. You'll see." Tommy remembers him saying that maybe a year ago. Tommy almost always held his piss all through the night, especially if he was in the loft. He didn't want to climb down the affixed loft ladder all tired-like and make his way outside. And Ma didn't want him pissin' out the window like Pa would do some nights. The next day, everyone would have to step around the mud on the bare ground on the barn side of the house below the loft window. Mawma detested that.

But Tommy didn't mean to fall asleep on the couch tonight. He just got too tired. He had been watching the stars fall with his face against the glass window with his cupped hand shielding his eyes from the lantern light inside. He and Pawpa stepped outside again maybe twenty minutes after the thud for just a minute or so. To listen and to look up again. The shower continued. But everything was quiet. Even in the cornfield.

As Tommy was drifting off, he saw Pawpa tend the small fire in the woodstove. Some unknown minutes later, when Tommy last opened his eyes before sleep took him for good, Pawpa was again leaning his forehead against the window glass, staring into the distance. He was up most of the night already, and daylight couldn't be that far off. Would he sleep at all tonight? That would make him dead tired tomorrow. Maybe take his afternoon rest early. There was one more streak of a meteor. And then another large one, colorful. Pawpa's jaw slacked into that rediscovered smile, and Tommy relaxed into sleep.

* * *

Tommy was good about waking up on time. Years ago, when they had chickens, the rooster made it very easy. After morning chores and after Mawma and Ma's—and then just Ma's—breakfast, it would be time to get to schooling. He missed the daily frying of bacon, the buttered bread, and the sound of eggs cracking into the oiled skillet. The sights and smells and tastes of breakfast made returning to the house after barn chores delightful. He loved Ma. He loved Mawma. Every day a good breakfast. But the chickens were long gone.

At least he still had Pawpa. Good Pawpa. Tommy smiled as he rubbed his eyes before standing up from the couch. This morning, Pawpa was snoring hard in the bedroom. The mid-November sun had broken the horizon, brightening the room. Rule was you don't piss in the pot if morning had broken. Tommy got up and set a two-inch thick piece of mesquite over the smoldering woodstove coals, before heading to the door. The shotgun remained beside it where Pawpa left it, leaning against the wall. Tommy stopped, leaned to the window, and looked out on the farmstead. Could something still be out there? He looked at the corner of the barn that was visible. At the well. The outhouse. The graveyard grove in the distance. And at the packed earth becoming a trace of wagon tracks at the far corner of the cornfield. He squinted at the cornfield. Nothing there, and he had to piss. Tommy looked over his shoulder to the bedroom. Beyond the open door was Pawpa, clothed and snoring above the covers. No boots. Socks in need of darning. Tommy turned the handle and pushed open the door. He stepped out, looking around the stead and listening before leaving the door just barely ajar.

He stepped onto the packed earth at the front of the house. It had been a strange night, and now Tommy was outside and alone. The outhouse was twenty yards away, behind a mesquite tree not far from the cornfield. Tommy looked all around again before heading off along the little path to the outhouse. As he hurried, he was watching for huisache and burrs and any thorny thing that was everywhere in South Texas. All the while, he was also glancing at the cornfield to his side, looking for anything. He even shot a look up to the bright sky. No meteors. At the outhouse he opened its door just a bit and peeked in to be sure nothing was there.

Business done, he pushed open the outhouse door and headed back to the house. That's when he saw it. Tommy froze. Something wasn't right in the cornfield. Maybe five and six rows in, there was a

THE CREAKLING

place where maybe eight stalks of corn used to stand. Something had removed them. Or broke them down. He couldn't tell. He bet himself it was from that thud last night. Tommy shot his look to the house door some fifteen yards away. Ajar just as he left it. He breathed in. "You're a man, now, Tommy," he said to himself. "Even Pawpa said so. Called me 'sir.'" And so, Tommy Jones Calhoun approached the cornfield in the direction of the missing cornstalks. He kept quiet. Kept looking about.

At the edge of the field and with the backs of his hands, he separated two stalks and stepped through, giving another quick glance back to the house. Stepping past the second row, there was a little rustle of corn leaves with a light gust of the morning breeze. Tommy paused and peered. Three rows farther ahead was the place. Something was there. Something not right. He twisted his head for a different look. It was some viny plant the color of red onion. It had grown over several crumpled stalks. It was almost glossy. Something he'd never seen. He bit his lower lip and looked back toward the house barely visible through the stalks. "It's just a plant, Tommy," he said to himself. Steeled, he moved through the next three rows and then took his stand at the edge of the six-foot wide and two-foot tall wonder in his cornfield.

The twisted, dense vine had red-purple leaves on purplish stems from which dozens of lighter-colored shoots twisted around fallen cornstalks. Some had penetrated into them. Other, thicker shoots—roots—had pierced the dark earth. Still more shoots had travelled out over the earth toward other stalks and other rows. The mass of it all was centered on a three-foot-wide depression in the soil. It was from there that the thickest of the vines began. Tommy stiffened. Nothing could grow that fast from last night.

"Pawpa!" he shouted without thinking as he bolted homeward through the stalks. Heart and mind racing, he called again as he left the field: "Pawpa! I found the thud!"

Boots in hand and wincing, Pawpa met him at the door. "Tommy!"

"It's a purple plant in the cornfield! From the storm!"

Pawpa looked to the cornfield. Opposite the outhouse, a stalk in the first row was cracked over mid-height. So was another one behind it. "Is that from your runnin'?"

Tommy looked back at the stalks he broke over. "Aw! Yes, Pawpa. But there's something passing strange deeper in there." He was pointing and starting a fast walk back to the cornfield.

"Let me put my boots on, Tommy."

* * *

"Well that's the damnedest thing."

"I know, Pawpa."

After another several seconds looking over the vine, Pawpa took a pained knee and leaned closer.

"Maybe not touch it, Pawpa." Tommy offered. "Like the poison oak or worse."

"I know it. I ain't touchin' nothin."

There was another light morning gust. The leaves rustled.

"Look at that." Pawpa pointed quick to a twist of vine. "Did ya see that shoot sprout out all quick like?"

Tommy took a knee beside his grandfather. "That one?"

"Yes. Look at it."

The light-purple shoot was still moving, coiling around the splintered shaft of a fallen cornstalk. Then, after a tightening, it stopped moving.

"The damnedest thing, Pawpa."

Pawpa bit his lip.

"There's another one," Tommy said quickly and with a point. One row over, a slightly larger sprout flapped against the rich black earth and poked into it before tightening and stopping its movement.

"Nothin' grows this fast."

"I know it, Pawpa."

Pawpa shook his head. With a little wince, he stood up. And Tommy did, too. "Go get the hand spade from the barn and your pail. We'll cut a piece of it. A piece with a leaf, a bit of vine stem, and a shoot. You'll take it to the sheriff. He's in town this part of the week. It's Thursday, right."

"Yes, sir."

"Take it to him. Tell him everything," Pawpa tightened a moment. "You can tell Sheriff Cartwright *anything*, Tommy." He looked down on him the way he could sometimes. "You hear me, Tommy?"

"I do, sir." Tommy said, looking up to his grandfather.

Pawpa set his hand on Tommy's shoulder. "That's good, Tommy. I know you'll remember that. Tell Cartwright *anything*." He gave a tight smile.

Tommy looked back at the vine. "What if it keeps on growin', Pawpa."

"We'll burn it," Pawpa replied quickly. "But not anytime soon. It risks the rest of the crop." He looked up to the morning sky. "I should'a had the Bronson brothers come last week with their combine."

"I know it, Pawpa," Tommy replied. "But it was right to hope for a little rain this week to plump up them corn."

"Maybe." Pawpa bit his lip again. "Let's get to it, now."

Tommy did.

* * *

Tommy Jones Calhoun was in his fast walk along the trace toward town. But it was a different kind of fast walk, not like the kind when he was late for school. And he wasn't late. Pawpa wanted him to see the sheriff first thing. And then check again at lunch if the sheriff wasn't there first thing. After school even if need be. Today, his front teeth and tongue held his bottom lip. He and Pawpa did that. Family trait or something when things were serious. His fingers tightly gripped the rim of his pail and, after every half-minute or so, he'd look down into the pail to see if the red-onion-colored vine had grown any. It never did. Even so, he kept his cramping fingers pinched at the pail's rim. When the cramping got up some, he'd switch off to his other hand.

"I can stitch both right and left," Ma said one time on the couch. Her work, a quilt, was over her lap. Tommy was leaning at her side. "The family arthritis ain't too much," she added, flexing her fingers and switching the threaded needle to her other hand.

"Your Ma's something special," Mawma then said, shucking corn at the kitchen prep table. Tommy remembered that moment for the first time ever as he kept on hastening along the trace. He slept under that quilt. Almost every night since forever. Mawma loved Ma. So did Tommy.

He checked the pail again. No growth, and the color of the vine was fading. Dulling. Maybe it had shrunk, too. But he kept his finger pinch near as he could to the rim. A mile from town, the trace ran alongside Little Creek for maybe fifty yards. He set the pail down and knelt, bringing his lips to the narrow, inch-deep run of water and sucked up some. He often did that to or from school. But the little drought had his lips touching the dark silt. And he had to tongue-spit that out. At least it wasn't sulfury. Little Creek had good water. If only the farmstead was here. A mile closer to town. Good water. But too much caliche for a good farm. The farmstead up past the rise had better soil.

He wiped his lips and stood up. The slope of the bank had him correct his step, and his foot hit the pail, knocking it over and casting the piece of vine out and onto the earth. Tommy stopped himself just before touching it to return it to the pail. He looked around and took a mesquite stick and tried to flip the vine back into the pail. It flopped out, so he stabbed it a bit against the earth and with the puncturing keeping it on the stick he scraped it back into the pail. Then he looked at the tip of the stick. A purplish smear was there. He tensed up and looked down at the earth where he had punctured the vine. He had made a little hole in the moist, dark earth. After a long moment considering what he had done, he dropped the stick and went on with the plan. He didn't know what else to do.

THE CREAKLING

* * *

Even if you were missing four fingers, the Main Street businesses of Little Lavaca could be counted on two hands. That was one of Pa's jokes. At the far end was the little municipal building and halfway down Main Street was the intersection leading in one direction to the schoolhouse, church, and livery and in the other direction to several in-town houses, the bathhouse, and after a good mile farther, the Knapp farmstead. William "Billy-Boy" Simms was leaving his family's little mercantile just as Tommy was entering town. The Simms had two rooms upstairs of the mercantile for Billy-Boy and the mister, and a nice in-town house for the missus. She had tea and coffee in a parlor. Tommy stepped inside that house once and even saw the parlor, but he couldn't go any farther in—on account of his dirty shoes. Billy-Boy made that very clear—on account of his mother.

"Hey, Billy-Boy!" Tommy called. "You should see this!" Tommy was pointing down toward his pail with a wide-eyed, tooth-baring shake of his head.

"Very bad lunch again?" was Billy-Boy's response. But he looked interested.

"You saw the stars last night, right?"

"Who didn't?" Billy-Boy said, walking toward him. "They rang the church bell maybe five minutes."

Billy-Boy was of normal weight and then just a pound or two or few heavier. But he could still run fast and climb good and you didn't want to challenge him if you were his age—and not because his Pa had a business and some money in town. It was because Billy-Boy had some real smarts about him and he actually popped an older boy in the nose when he was in fourth grade. He was twelve-and-a-half, now. He went to services. He was mostly always honest. One day, when he and Tommy were skipping stones over Big Creek, Billy-Boy said that he would start being called "William" once he turned thirteen, and that Tommy had to call him that. Tommy agreed. Tommy said he should start being called "Tomas" at thirteen, too, but Billy-Boy said that Tommy was only saying that because of what he just said. And he was right.

They were alone on the street that morning, except for Old Man Jenkins unlocking his Shave and Bathhouse and stepping in and turning his window sign to "OPEN". Billy-Boy was getting close. "If you say you've got some shootin' star but you only got your potato, I'll smack you upside your head and steal it so you got nothing for lunch!"

Tommy grinned wide. "I *have* got one of them stars, William! Something from it—I really do. Pawpa and I think one hit our cornfield last night, and this sprouted up!" He tipped the pail toward Billy-Boy. "Don't touch it. It might be real poisonous. My Pawpa says so."

Billy-Boy peered in. He twisted his look. "Naw. That just some dyin' fancy plant." He started reaching toward it.

"I'm dead serious, Billy!" Tommy said, pulling the pail away. "Something's passing strange about it all."

Billy-Boy behaved himself. "Alright, Tommy. You say it's from the sky. What are you going to do?"

"I'm bringin' it to Sheriff Cartwright right now," Tommy began. "Pawpa and I saw it grow—you could *see* it grow. That's how fast it grows. Pawpa will burn it tomorrow if it grows more in the cornfield." Then Tommy got manly serious, "Now William, you gotta keep this all quiet until Sheriff Cartwright sees it and tells us what to do. Pawpa don't want people coming over for curiosity's sake. It could be poisonous. So you gotta keep it quiet."

Billy-Boy looked Tommy over. "All right, Tommy. I'll keep it quiet."

"Good. And I'll tell you first what the sheriff says to do."

Billy-Boy looked at Tommy's flat pockets and then at his pail. "So is that what yer eatin' for lunch today, Tommy?" he asked with a smirk.

THE CREAKLING

"I was hopin' to ask for some pieces of bread here and there. We plumb forgot about it all—lunch—as me and Pawpa tried figurin' what to do. And I left all stupid about it."

"I'll go heist you a couple older apples. My pa won't care about that if he sees it. Prob'ly not care, at least." And with that Billy-Boy headed back to the mercantile.

"I owe you again," Tommy said as he headed on down Main Street.

And that's when Tommy saw her. Loretta Mae Knapp. Walking with Ella Jane Stubbs and that silly little Henry girl, Ingrid. Loretta had her pail at the bend of her elbow. Tommy loved how she'd do that. Carrying her pail that way. Ella Jane was talking about whatever she loved to talk about that day and Loretta was nodding with her toothy smile. Tommy so loved her teeth. They were far worse than his. If he could love her teeth, he thought he could love her for anything. He knew that. He was watchin' her. The Henry girl tapped at Loretta and said something up near her ear and then pointed at Tommy. Tommy looked down to his walk and kept on. His pinch was cramping, so he switched it. They were all getting closer together. They were crossing paths at the intersection of town. He was looking down even though Pawpa called Tommy "Sir" last night. That steeled him. He looked up as he approached the three girls heading toward school. Loretta was wearing her pale yellow dress with a pattern. He liked that one. Warm and bright like Loretta. He had to slow down in his head and in his walk, and he did. Both.

"Did you see the stars last night?" is what he asked out. He was looking at none of them so as not to just stare at Loretta.

"I did!" Loretta said quick-like.

And with that, they had spoken again to each other. She answered what he asked. Like before. He held back his happiness. He chose a glance at the Henry girl and then chose a glance at Ella Jane—so no one could think that he'd be only be wanting to look at Loretta, whom he then started looking at softly. He couldn't take his eyes off her. "I thought the night sky was as beautiful as you, Loretta." He said that! Softly even. He didn't know how he said it—he just did! But all he could do then was look down. He just stopped, and looked at the packed dry dirt of the intersection road.

The two other girls giggled. Tommy shook his head. "I didn't mean it like that!" was all he got out.

The girls giggled on. Maybe even Loretta was giggling some as they took up their walk toward the schoolhouse past the Main Street intersection. They were speaking, too. Tommy twisted his downturned look toward them. Loretta Mae was just then glancing over her shoulder back at him. Barely open tight smile over her bad teeth. So beautiful. And she quickly looked away forward just as Tommy himself started to quickly look away.

He breathed in. He had called her beautiful.

Nowhere now to look and go but forward. Pawpa said as much earlier. "This plan all sounds right, yes? So do what I say, Tommy. You must. Take it to Sheriff Cartwright." And that's what Tommy was doing. And the little municipal building with a boardwalk porch all official-like and with some signage by the door was not too far away. Tommy headed toward it. Two storefronts closer, at the Farmers Shoppe, Mr. McPherson brought out his stool and set it behind his outside worktable near the shop's door. No one worked harder in town than Mr. McPherson. "Knew both caliche and black earth like the back of his hand," Pawpa said. McPherson gave Tommy a nod and Tommy liked that, so he gave the same nod back with his smile before looking and continuing forward. He was a man, now. He knew it. And the municipal building was just a few seconds away.

Tommy Jones Calhoun stepped up onto the boardwalk and tried the doorknob, but the door was locked. He knocked and peeked through the glass beyond the little gap of the curtain. Nothing in the two-room and one-jailcell building. But he waited and then knocked harder. Nothing.

* * *

THE CREAKLING

Schooling had just begun. Students had their clean slates and pieces of chalk on their desktops and their lunch pails or lunch sacks under their desks. Today, Tommy kept his pail between his feet. He had pressed a piece of paper just into it, as if it were a shield against flies that might try after some meat. The contents could then remain secret, so long as Billy-Boy kept his mouth shut. He shouldn't have shown him anything. Pawpa said keep it all quiet. Even so, Miss Koehler was always on the lookout both for mischief and for anything out of place. Teacher had to be that way, what with John and chubby Edwin and sometimes others or even Tommy himself disobeyin' some class rule or another. She kept all the boys straight. Girls too. Had to. Good parents liked that about good teachers. Keepin' 'em straight all alone in the schoolhouse. His stomach was growling and he thought about taking bites out of one of the two apples on his desktop when Miss Koehler turned back to the class after writing "Meteor Shower" big on the board. He should have eaten one of the apples before class, but it was too late now.

"Tommy Calhoun? Why aren't those apples in your pail?"

Tommy didn't know what to do. All the students, ages six to fourteen, were turning their looks to him. He was afraid.

Billy-Boy spoke up quick-like, "It's 'cause what's in his pail, Miss Koehler." Looks turned over to him. "He's got some little smoked bass his Pawpa caught yesterday at the pond way up Little Creek. Wants to keep the apples away. Doesn't want them to smell. Bad enough he already smells like sulfur! Can't have his apples smelling, too!"

The classroom laughed. Miss Koehler struck in. "William Simms! What did I say about talkin' about anyone's smell? That is not polite public talk. I do not want to hear that from you again."

"Yes, Ma'am," he said, looking down.

Snickering subsided with her scan of the room and the faces in it. Miss Koehler then spoke to Tommy with a softer tone. "Tommy, you know there's no food on desks until luncheon,"

Tommy could only nod.

"Bring those two apples to my desk until it's time." And that was all she said before turning a bit to the board and pointing to the words she wrote. "Now, who can tell me what the word "Meteor" actually means? Anyone?"

William "Billy-Boy" Simms had just saved Tommy. Another debt. Tommy looked at William, who winked in his little smirk at him. Tommy nodded and then looked at Loretta Mae looking at him and then at Billy-Boy and then at Tommy's pail. She straightened up a bit and looked at the board, on which Miss Koehler was adding the word "Atmosphere." Loretta looked like she didn't want to move, but she looked out the corner of her eye at Tommy still looking at her. Tommy looked down.

* * *

It was a nice day, so Miss Koehler let lunch be outside. She liked sitting under one of the post oaks along Big Creek, which ran behind the school. She'd bring her little blanket and eat her lunch, occasionally correcting kids from afar as they ate or ran or climbed or played or said something in some way she didn't like. Sometimes young Mr. Danes came over from the livery, where he labored. He was a strong man recently come from Kentucky, Miss Koehler told the class one day after lunch. But Miss Koehler also made sure that he kept his shirt buttoned all the way up, what with the young girls around and all. He was almost as tall as Pawpa and had thick hair. Sometimes, he'd sit at the edge of teacher's blanket and have his own luncheon, but he wasn't here, today.

With his small, bruised, and too-soft apples eaten quickly, Tommy wiped his maw and then steeled himself again. Pail in his grip, he walked up to his teacher sitting prim under her post oak on her little blanket. "Miss Koehler?"

"Yes, Tommy?" She was still preparing her lunch beside her.

"My Pawpa says I must tell something to Sheriff Cartwright today."

"He did?"

THE CREAKLING

"Yes, ma'am. Pawpa thinks someone's stealin' our tools from the barn, but maybe it's just Pawpa's memory about where he put things, but it has been three tools, now. He wants to know if anyone else had been stolen from. And sheriff wasn't in this morning before school, so Pawpa said I would need check for him at lunch."

"Sorry to hear this, Tommy." She looked up to him. "Well you best get on, then," she said with a quick smile before turning back down to her halved roll with four slices of sweet onion placed on each half. The halves were buttered.

Tommy thought about how good butter was. "Yes, Ma'am," he said as she opened a small jar of mustard. Another nice, whole roll, some more butter on an unfolded piece of wax paper, and the rest of the onion remained in her own lunch pail.

"Anything else, Tommy?" Miss Koehler asked. She had stopped preparing her lunch. She had a tired smile on her a face.

"No, ma'am," Tommy said fast as he turned away.

Tommy wasn't even hardly-trained at lying, because he usually didn't do it, but he did it in that moment just fine. He made his way fast for Main Street as other children about him were eating or laughing or playing or climbing trees in the scant half-acre that separated Big Creek, the schoolhouse, and the Little Lavaca Livery.

That's when Loretta walked right up to Tommy as he was nearing the limit of the half-acre. "Whatcha doin', Tommy Jones?" Her nose was scrunched.

Tommy stopped and looked around fast-like for anyone other than Loretta that might be looking at them. Ella Jane and Ingrid were looking away in their own almost-bashful smiles at each other. They were happy about Loretta suddenly walking up to Tommy, maybe. Even so, Tommy kept on searching. He found Billy-Boy, who was shrugging and shaking his head. It wasn't him that sent Loretta to him. Tommy looked at one more person. Miss Koehler. Oblivious. She was chewing on a big bite and leaning slightly against the tree trunk. Eyes closed for a long moment as Miss sometimes did at lunch.

"Tommy? You got something in yer pail, don't you?" Loretta asked serious-like, reaching just a bit toward it.

Tommy tried to remember how to steel himself as a man, but he failed and only worried she might somehow touch the plant. "Stay away, Loretta!" is all he stated as he started on again at a quick walk away from the half-acre.

Two moments later, he looked back at Loretta standing at the edge. She was looking down. Sad-faced. Tommy frighted a bit about what he just said and did. "Not like *that*, Loretta Mae!" he called back before taking up an even quicker pace along Main Street. Looking ahead, he saw a horse hitched at the little municipal building. Sheriff Cartwright's horse. He shifted his grip on his pail. Glancing back, he saw Loretta Mae Knapp walking back to her two friends, who joined up on either side of her. They were all looking at each other heart-felt or something. Tommy was no man yet, hurting her like he just did. He even made her friends feel somehow sad. So he didn't speak right at all to her. He wanted to go back, explain it some, and never let it happen again. But he was on a mission. And that was somehow easier steeling. So he headed for the municipal building and the sheriff inside.

* * *

The door was unlocked, so Tommy just went on in, glancing at the empty cell, at the records room beyond an open doorway at the back of the building, and then at Sheriff Cartwright looking at Tommy from the main room's desk. Papers were in the sheriff's left hand. They were alone.

Sheriff Cartwright was maybe ten-years younger than Pawpa, but more weathered. "All that time in the saddle makin' sure right stayed right as right was, countryside," Pawpa once said, looking down on Tommy the way he could sometimes. Tommy remembered that then. He turned to close the door behind him. "Sheriff," he said, man-like, with a scan out the window before turning around and facing the man. "There's a problem at our farm."

"Alright, Mister Calhoun," the sheriff replied flatly and without moving. "Let's hear it."

Tommy approached the desk. His free hand was pointing at his pail. "It's something serious, Sheriff. Something came from heaven."

The sheriff tensed the slightest bit. He raised an eyebrow. "What's that?" he asked, still speaking flatly.

"I have some plant from heaven, Sheriff." Tommy said matter-of-factly.

The sheriff snorted lightly. "Is that so. From that storm last night, Tommy? You're joking."

"No, sir," Tommy Jones Calhoun continued. "And I'm serious as fact. And Pawpa said I could say *anything* to you, and that you'd have to figure it out. It's something bad from heaven, Sheriff, and I can ask you anything."

That's when the sheriff twitched ever-so-slightly and took almost pale despite all his weathering. He dipped his head slow-like a bit and took a big breath. "What's in the pail, Tommy?"

Tommy slowed down, because Sheriff Cartwright looked strong and fragile at the same time. Brittle or something. Tommy tightened his jaw as he set the pail atop the sheriff's desk, holding the pail down with one hand at the rim as he removed the piece of paper that concealed its contents. He then tilted it just a bit toward the sheriff, revealing the drying, somewhat decolored section of vine and leaf and shoot and root that were all much shriveled in the bottom quarter of the pail. "This is growing too fast on the farm. There's already a huge patch of it. It's somethin' not recognized by Pawpa, and we heard it hit the cornfield during the storm. We thought it was a bear or mountain lion or somethin' pouncing late last night at first. Found it this morning, a wide patch of it creeping over many stalks of corn. But it's from the storm, Sheriff. And you can see it growin'. Growin' fast."

The sheriff looked at his gripped papers in his hand and then set them down on the desk next to his leather satchel and then, with a little lean, he peered into the pail. He barely moved for a few seconds as he pursed his lips and tightened his brows. He then picked up the wooden letter opener on the desktop. "It's some thick, purplish vine." He raised a brow. "I ain't never seen this, Tommy." He started fishing into the pail with the opener.

"Don't touch it, sheriff," Tommy began with the littlest pull away. "It might be poisonous. We haven't touched it—just dug it up with a trowel."

"Mmm. That's best," the sheriff said, easing up. He then worked slower, reaching the wooden letter opener back in, poking at the leaf, and then flipping it over. He pressed the tip of the opener into the overturned leaf at the bottom of the pail. "Tommy? I'm no farmer. But I've lived either here in our county or what's now Duval all my life." He was studying the plant. "I've never seen anything like this. Never heard of it, neither." He withdrew the opener from the pail and set it on the desk. He rubbed his chin one long moment. "You said you could see it move?"

"Yes, sir."

"How fast?"

"You saw that shoot that's dried up in the pail?"

"Yes."

"We watched 'em just like that one stretch out of a vine stem and latch onto cornstalks. It could coil maybe two inches around something before tightening into a rest. Real fast-like. Into the soil, too. Stretching and tightening up before stopping. Unnatural. But that one's dried up small."

The sheriff looked at Tommy for a long moment. "Tommy Jones Calhoun, you'd best not be lyin' to me."

"No, sir."

The sheriff exhaled. "Alright," he began. "I need to carry out a warrant in Big Lavaca, first thing tomorra. I'm leaving this hour. Right now. Already late. Other men joinin' me, there. I'm deputizin' four of them. It'll take a day to do it all, but I'll come back, Tommy. Tomorra very late afternoon or in the night. Then or first thing

Saturday, I'll plan on headin' on out to your farmstead." He paused just a moment. "And, Tommy, I'm taking your pail with that vine-thing with me."

"Yes, sir," Tommy said, pressing the paper cover just into the pail again. He slid the pail a few inches closer to the sheriff and then released it. That was the first time all day that his pail had been out of his care—except for that long moment when he had to place his apples on teacher's desk.

"I'll show it around—to my deputies, any farmer I meet, and even to that librarian they have in Lavaca. Someone might know something. Maybe the storm brought this somewhere else, too—if it *is* from above. And I'll give McPherson a look at it before I go."

Tommy looked at the sheriff a long moment. It was a good plan, but there was something else that needed saying. Tommy remembered that he was a man now, and that he could say anything to the sheriff. Thinking about that helped him steel himself one more time. "Sheriff. I have to ask you somethin' else. Somethin' serious."

"Alright, Tommy," the sheriff again said flatly. "What is it."

"How did they die, Sheriff? I just can't remember."

Sheriff didn't move. Tommy didn't like that.

"Do you know who I mean, Sheriff?" he asked again.

"I do, Tommy." Sheriff was intent on Tommy. "You're talking about your parents."

"Yes, sir."

"People get fevers, sometimes. *Bad* fevers."

Tommy knew that. So he responded quick-like. "Pawpa says I was in the pit for that long time—part of two days—because the fever could spread."

"That's right, Tommy. It can. And it did. It took your Ma and Pa."

"No one else got that fever, Sheriff."

"That's right, Tommy. Your Pawpa stopped that spread. He knew what he had to do." The sheriff kept his look on Tommy.

Tommy thought some of that must be true, but there remained something dark and unsettled in his mind. So he kept at it. "But why don't I remember Ma being sick, Sheriff? She died first—Pawpa said—and I was in the pit by then. I was in the pit all overnight, too. Deep into next afternoon."

"Yes. Your grandfather kept you away from it all."

"But why did Pawpa have to *lock* me in? I was in darkness for so long. I tried pushing up the pit door more than once. Screamed screams no one heard. And I never even knew she was sick. How can you know at the start that it was so bad a fever that you needs lock people away from it?"

"There are bad fevers out there, Tommy."

Tommy started thinking, looking down hard. How could Pawpa have known at the earliest onset of some fever to keep him away so he couldn't even remember anything about it. That's what remained unsettled. And now Tommy knew what to ask. "What kind of fever *was* it?" he asked as he began staring, serious and grown-up-like at the sheriff, even with the sheriff staring right back at him.

"The yellow fever had been around these parts before."

There was a long pause as they held their looks at each other.

"Is that what it was, Sheriff? *Yellow* fever?"

Sheriff looked away. "Maybe."

And that's when Tommy knew the sheriff was lying. Tommy kept his mouth shut. Men have to, sometimes. To figure things. Or to keep things from being figured. And Tommy was trying to figure why he could tell Cartwright anything if he'd only lie about it if he did. So he responded in kind, not sayin' what was truly in his thoughts. "Sheriff, whatever *fever* you want to call it took my Ma."

There was some moment of silence. "That it did, Tommy. That it did." Then, finally looking back at Tommy, the sheriff started speaking so genuine-like and kindly despite all the weather of his face. "And I am truly sorry. I am. And your Pawpa stopped all that fever from spreading any farther. That's the God's honest truth, Tommy. The God's honest truth. Your Pawpa stopped it. Saved you. And himself."

THE CREAKLING

"Yes, sir," Tommy said, looking down a moment—like a boy would after being told to accept something he might rather not accept. But Tommy did it with purpose. With head slightly bowed, he looked up serious-like and slow at Sheriff Cartwright. They had lied to end any talk of it all. Because now Tommy knew what Pawpa and the sheriff had kept unspoken. Why talk of it? Little Lavaca—little Tommy's world—would never need know what his Pa done.

Sheriff nodded very slowly as he held his kind look at Tommy. And after that, the sheriff just stood up and placed his papers into the leather satchel on the desk. "Now I got a warrant to serve in Big Lavaca, Tomas Jones. Could turn real bad. But I have every intention of bein' at your place tomorra late or first thing Saturday."

"Thank you, Sheriff Cartwright," Tommy said flatly. "I am obliged."

The sheriff gave no response. He had a cap-and-ball revolver in a cross-reaching holster at his left hip. He unlocked the gun cabinet standing against the wall and took out from it one of its two rifles along with a twenty-round box of forty-four caliber cartridges. He locked the cabinet back up and just stood there looking at it a moment. "Maybe you best get back to doin' what Samuel Jones would have you do. He's a good man, Tomas."

"Yes, sir," Tommy said. And that's when he saw it. The wooden letter opener had a slightest stain of purple at its very tip. Tommy squinted. And there was the littlest strand of light-purple fiber on it. Maybe the smallest new sprouting? Or maybe just a fiber from the leaf. He turned to the door and opened it. "Best look close at that opener of yours, Sheriff. Maybe add it to the pail heading to Big Lavaca, too." And with that, he closed the door on a trustworthy liar heading out on some other mission across all the mesquite and huisache brushland. Makin' sure right stayed right as right was, countryside. Way down inside, was Tommy any different? He would also keep quiet about what he now knew. And he didn't like what he knew one bit. But he had done what Pawpa knew needed doin'. And now he needed to bring it all back to Pawpa! Good, strong Pawpa. And to ask specific questions that maybe only Pawpa could answer.

* * *

Tommy walked with purpose, turning at the Main Street intersection heading behind the mercantile and past some of the in-town houses. By doing so, he'd avoid any looks or distractions that might come from the schoolyard if lunch ran late. Worse would be if Miss Koehler herself saw him and asked of him something or anything— or even beckoned him back into schooling. He was barely a liar with her, and had now doubled his genuine and serious experience in lying in a mere fifteen minutes. He knew it was better to side-step all that fact and move on. He was also moving with a half-smile, both because he had carried out a real mission and because he knew that he was now on a bit of the way Loretta Mae Knapp walked every day to and from the school they shared. Something about those facts made him happy.

Having passed two houses along her road, he found the cut-through he had in mind. It was the fenceless open yard of an in-town property he and Billy-Boy ran through once or thrice some time back. Beyond it was a path heading back to the road that led to his own way out of town. After a hundred yards along that road, he'd turn right onto the familiar trace that led home to Pawpa.

And so, Tommy trespassed the house's property at a run. Boys did such things, and they usually got away with it. Few cared about boys running around. But today, Tommy was both a boy and a man. He was puissant! He had stared down a sheriff! And in doing so, he had learned the unspoken truth of it all. The truth about his Pa. And what Pawpa had to do about it, being countryside and all. He also knew something from the heavens. And because of it—and maybe for safety's sake—he even twisted the truth to his teacher about his reason to see the sheriff. He twisted it all, even though preacher said you shouldn't twist the truth. But he did twist it. Like Sheriff had done. Like good Pawpa had done ever since. So, Tommy had to get

THE CREAKLING

home to share it all with Pawpa. He'd be proud of Tommy. And what's more, Tommy was very much in love with someone he couldn't afford to set his mind on again just yet. Even so, he was grinning about it all as he left his trespass, because he knew that he would be a happy man, come what may. Tommy felt alive something like never before.

"Hey, Tommy!"

It was Loretta, running after him across the yard—running in that pale yellow dress of hers. She was smiling.

Tommy smiled all surprised back at her. They stopped several feet from each other on the start of the path back to Tommy's way out of town.

"What are you doing, here, Loretta Mae?"

"Followin' you," she began. "Still wanting to know what's so secret about that old pail you're no longer carrying." She scrunched her cute little nose. "You already lost its handle—did the bottom now fall out, Tommy? Making you finally throw it away?"

For a moment Tommy didn't move. Loretta Mae Knapp was talking to him. And he was in love with her. What's more, now that he didn't have the pail, he didn't have to keep her away from him for safety or something. He somehow put together a whole sentence that made sense of the entirety of all. "I know you kid, Loretta, but I didn't throw it away. I just now gave it to the sheriff all serious-like. He's taking it to Big Lavaca, because of what's in it. The storm brought something wrong to our farm, Loretta. And part of it I put in the pail."

She took a step closer. "You mean something fell from the sky last night onto your farm?"

"Yes. Some plant that's growing wicked-fast in our cornfield. You can see it grow."

"Tommy, you can't see no plant grow."

"I know. But we can see this one."

She stood still a moment, except for the bitin' of her bottom lip. Maybe she was thinking over it all. After a quick look over her shoulder, she said, "Are you asking me to go see it with you, Tommy Jones?"

It happened again, that nervousness that made Tommy think it best just not to move or speak, but just to look down. He tensed up.

"I know that's not what you meant, Tommy," she began after a moment. "I was just playing about going there with you."

That's when Tommy realized she didn't know he was nervous, and he didn't at all want her to get nervous because of it, so he breathed in and looked up at her. "Loretta, I'm just nervous something special, that's all. You're talkin' to me—and I like it that you're talkin' to me. I just always say things stupid." Almost without knowing, he took a short step closer to her.

"I want to go see it on your farm, Tommy Jones," she replied, with the slightest lean forward. "I really do."

Some yet-unknown emotion fell over him. It wasn't that ecstasy word he had heard about. But it was something more or different than joy. But a serious concern brought his thinking straight back after that all-inside feeling. So he just let out a sharp laugh. "Loretta, you can't go with me, right now. You *can't*. You've got school, and lunch must be over by now. Koehler'll report you tardy or even truant. A note will reach your home today or tomorrow for sure. You don't want that."

She wagged a finger and scrunched her cute little nose again, exposing her bad teeth. "Ingrid and Ella and I made up a finest plan, Tommy!" She looked around and quieted down a bit. "I would hurry to the girls' outhouse when no one was in it and Ingrid and Ella would be sure to be standing up and looking there where Miss could see them when I would then go running out straight away and toward my road home without stopping come what may. Miss would look up for sure when that outhouse door slammed shut hard, and she'd see me running. Plan was that even if Miss called for me, I'd keep on running. She didn't. At the same time, Ella would come up to Miss under her oak tree and tell her that I was getting a period for the first time. Miss Koehler would believe her, because Ella has them almost regular-like, because she's thirteen. And then Ingrid would come up to Miss as well and say if asked anything that I felt all knotted up all morning." Loretta was grinning as Tommy stopped moving again. "It was all a finest plan, Tommy!"

Tommy didn't say anything, but this time it was for some different reason. When any female spoke or hinted at that woman thing that happens regular-like weeks apart, boys and men just don't make comments on it, Pawpa taught him, because it was the mystery of the creation of life. "Eve's bloody garden," chubby Edwin once said. Tommy's mind was stuck on all that.

She half-turned away. "Well if you don't want me to give you some company, Tommy. . . .." She looked out of the corner of her eye at him with a little raise of her brows.

He could hardly say anything, so he just said the truth. "I do want you to, Loretta. I do." Somehow, he had said something right again, because she smiled and turned toward him.

* * *

They were four feet apart, walking beside each other on the separate wheel traces toward Tommy's farmstead. Tommy was walking the left trace, and he wasn't used to that. But that's how they were lined up as they turned off the road just outside of town. And it was better that way, because he'd know every step along Loretta's trace. He could warn her of poor footing or some new thorny huisache or mesquite growth that he hadn't kicked away dead enough.

"This used to be a real wagon road, Loretta," he began, looking up the trace. "During our wagon rides to church before my ma and pa died, I used to sit on a quilt my Mawma made. Regular-like to church back then. And on many Saturdays, too, into town. But it's still easy-walking. I keep our path good and clear."

"I got a new blanket last Christmas," Loretta said. "And my ma taught me how to knit and darn and sew, and I made a small quilt over summer."

That made Tommy happy. Loretta had warm blankets against the cold.

Girls and boys are different, and Tommy and Loretta didn't say much as they walked, but they'd smile when they'd look at each other. And one smile can take up fifty yards of thoughts.

Three-quarters of a mile up the trace, Tommy thought of something specific to ask. "Your plan had you run home?"

She nodded.

"I've seen you run at recess. You're fast."

She smiled, keeping her look upon the trace. "I'm faster than any girl in school apart from Ella and Margret—but ol' Margie don't show up no more."

"Faster than some of the boys, too," Tommy added.

"*Most* of the boys," she said with a glance.

"You think you're faster than me?"

"I know it."

"I'm faster than you think, Loretta."

She stopped and so did Tommy. Loretta Mae Knapp was calculating with a squint in her eyes. "For fifty or a hundred yards, maybe," she began, "but you're too scrawny to last long runnin' fast, Tommy Jones!" She wagged a finger at him. "I'd beat ya!"

Tommy didn't like that. He wanted to yell at her that it wasn't his fault that he was scrawny and that they all died and that he now only had his old Pawpa and that the farm was only what it was and that his Pawpa was only what he was and that they only barely made it together, and that that's what made him too skinny. And that it wasn't his fault at all, because he tried—he really did. For a slightest moment, his right fist started clenching. But he remembered that he would be a happy man. He was puissant. It wasn't Loretta hurting him. He was looking down, and he promised himself right then and there that he would never again start to clench his fist like that against Loretta. Come what may.

"I didn't really mean it, Tommy," she said.

THE CREAKLING

He looked up at her with his soft smile. "All right, Suck-Tooth! See way up ahead where Little Creek runs near the trail? That's where I take a sip most days. Fresh creek water. Real sweet water. I'll race ya to it! Even let ya start runnin' first."

"I am thirsty," she said. Then, quick as a whip and pointing down at Tommy's feet, she added, "Snake!"

Tommy hopped back and looked down at nothing at the edge of the trace, but she was off running in that pale yellow dress of hers. And she was fast. But Tommy knew the entire trace and every dip and distortion in existence along its way, both this way and that. He bounded over to the right wheel trace yards behind Loretta. She had to look before her feet as she ran, what with the unfamiliar terrain and the thorny brush here and there threatening her exposed ankles and lower shins. In a flash, he was right behind her. "I can pass you anytime, Loretta!" he called out. He was leaning his head a bit, looking at her face as he ran.

"Not fair, Tommy!" she called out. "You know the path!"

He tried for a moment to cut across to the left trace to pass her, but the grasses and weeds between the tracks troubled his stride, so he kept just behind her along their right trace, enjoying being as fast as they could be together. William's apples fed him just enough! He knew he'd have to thank him again. "Anytime, Loretta! I could pass you!" he repeated with a big open smile on his face.

"Not fair!" She called again with a quick look back with her bad teeth bared as she ran. She was breathing harder.

They were nearing the place along Little Creek where Tommy would sip water. And that's when some look of fear came over her. She was wide-eyed, and staggering to a stop. Tommy managed to avoid bumping into her as he stepped into the grass between the wheel traces. They had almost touched. But that's when he saw what she was looking at. And he grew pale in his own seeing of it.

"Is that it, Tommy? That just can't be right."

The red-onion-colored vine was growing along the stretch of Little Creek where it ran almost alongside the trace. The vine stretched for some twenty feet in the water and along the creek bank, and, in places, it was bundled and twisted over itself as high as three feet. It was along the other side of the oak-shaded creek, too. It had even begun climbing up two post oaks, and it had spread out some into the brushland on the far side of the creek. On this side, some of it was only a few feet from the trace.

"That's where I spilled the vine out of the pail this morning, Loretta." He was breathing hard. "It just barely touched the ground. Just barely! Look at it all."

"It can't grow that fast." She was looking up and down the creek.

Tommy looked up the trace toward the farmstead. "No," he said weakly as his shoulders drooped.

In the distance, a half-mile closer to the farmstead, the land was tinged with the vine's color. It was spreading from the farm. Loretta saw it, too.

"You need to go, Loretta!"

"Tommy?"

"You need to warn the town! Tell them what's happening. Go! You shouldn't be here anyway!" And with that, he started at a sprint toward his farmstead.

"What are you gonna do?" she called.

"I need to find Pawpa!" he called without looking back. "Go away! Go home!"

* * *

Less than a half mile from the stead, Tommy came to a stop. The growth of the vine had spread through some of the brushland in front of him and to his right and left. He was breathing hard from a second run. The trace ahead remained clear, but the huisache and mesquite brushland on either side of the trace had some stretches of vine in it. And his side hurt. So he gripped it and stopped his breathing a moment. He was thirsty.

That's when he heard it. The creakling. The sound of slow-moving vines and their shoots stretching out and wrapping around

THE CREAKLING

and overtaking other life. Grasses. Brushland branches. Old oak trees. Anything. It was the sound of overtaken foliage becoming crumpled, dry, and brittle. Fed upon by some weird life. He gasped in his need of air. He forced himself quiet again. It was still there. The distant creakling of something spreading slowly, yet terribly too fast.

Maybe fifty feet in front of him was a five-foot stretch of vine nearly alongside the right trace. Still holding his side and recovering his breath, he walked fast up to it. The vine was a one-inch-thick offshoot of a larger twist of thicker vine several yards away in the brushland. Tommy took a knee and looked. A shoot leapt from a nub in the vine and then latched around a doveweed stem before tightening and tapping into it and then easing up. He saw another shoot wrap around a small clump of prairie grass. There was other creakling elsewhere. Almost everywhere elsewhere. Creakling all around.

Then Tommy saw something important. Only a couple of feet ahead of him, a sprout shot out onto the trace. It twisted and flapped at the packed, dry earth before pulling back, drying out and thinning in its retraction. "Bad soil," Tommy thought. "It can't spread on packed earth." He looked up. Maybe the trace was safe the entire way home.

A quail fluttered up not too far from him. He stood and watched it as its talons flexed and flexed again in its flight. There was a reddish-purple shoot hooked around one of its talons as it flapped away over the brushland before landing some fifty yards away. Tommy shook his head slowly and looked forward along the wagon trace clear of vine. But it was worse. Atop the low rise ahead was thicker vine in a twisted growth taller than the grasses in some places. And some was reaching up a few of the dozens of huisache brushes and mesquite trees. Beyond that rise would be the cornfield and his farmhouse. And Pawpa. Tommy started sprinting again.

The cornfield was packed with the vine. Overtaken. The largest vine stems were some five inches thick. And some of the twisted bundles were four or even five feet high. The soil beneath it all was cracked and parched. Only an occasional cornstalk remained standing. The rest were collapsed down and fed upon by sprouts and shoots growing into vine stems all their own. And there were leaves. Many wide, flat leaves splayed out along the vine. But the dirt roads and paths of the farmstead remained clear. Tommy was nearly spent, loping in his run as he turned the cornfield's corner and saw the small three-room farmhouse with his tall loft.

"No!" is all he could breathe out as he staggered to another stop.

While the front of the house was clear of vine, the side closest to the cornfield was overrun, with the vine creeping up the wall, even reaching a bit onto the roof. But something didn't look right at the front of the house. The glass pane window wasn't glossy. And it wasn't reflective. Nor dark. It was tinged with purple beyond it. The creakling was inside! So Tommy staggered back into a run toward the front door. "Pawpa!" he cried. "Pawpa!"

His heart was all apace as he again came to a stop, this time on the parched earth a few feet from the front of the house. He shook his head. Creakling vine and leaves and shoots were pressed against the glass window pane from the inside. Tommy looked about the door. Shoots had curled outward from the gap at the base of the door, latching onto the bottom of the door. Other sprouts were latching into the wood near the door's top.

"Pawpa!" Tommy cried out. Nothing. He looked along the packed earth toward the barn. It was clear of vine. He cupped his hands. "Pawpa!" he screamed. "Pawpa! Where are you!" He was spent of his air. He breathed hard and bent down, pressing his hands against his thighs.

That's when he heard it over his own breath and the creakling. It was his Pawpa's voice from inside the farmhouse. Scratchy. Frail. *"Tommy. Tommy."*

"Pawpa!" Tommy shouted full of sudden energy. He rushed to the door. He kept his feet from the shoots reaching out below and he looked at the handle. No purple tint. He pulled, but the door was

THE CREAKLING

stuck shut. Looking at the sprouts reaching through the gap at the top of the door, he cursed under his breath some word to God in heaven and then yanked for all his worth. He fell backward onto the dry earth as the door flew open. He flipped his look around himself, searching fast for any purple on him. Nothing. He hopped up and looked into the farmhouse. He stepped closer. The interior was a thicket of purplish vine, leaves, sprouts and shoots. Not much light made it through the house from the other side. He watched his step and everywhere as he moved slowly to the doorway of his home. Inside, the loft and spice rack and stove chimney were visible, although shoots and sprouts and small vines were latching into the wood walls. It was all a very slow and thickening crawl of vine inside. Through some of that thicket, he could see part of one of Pawpa's boots beside the couch. And just deeper in, on the couch, he could see Pawpa's socked foot, a sock in need of darning.

"*Tommy.*" And the socked foot twitched.

"I can't hardly see you, *Pawpa!*" Tommy started crying. "There's no way in, Pawpa. There's no way in! It's all packed!"

"*I had to . . ..*" Pawpa's voice was so dry and scratchy. "*Tommy.*"

"Figure it out!" Tommy thought hard, forcing himself to stop doing anything and just think. How to save Pawpa. The loft window. "Hold on, Pawpa! I'll save you!" And with that, Tommy was screeching and running fierce over the packed earth to the barn. He passed Big Waddle and So-Soda in the ox pen, standing as if nothing was happening. Tommy could see their wet trough was full. Pawpa had done that, too. "O *Pawpa!*" In the tool room, next to the old spare lumber bin was the farm's twelve-foot ladder—long enough for most things on the farmstead and perhaps just long enough to access the loft window fifteen feet up. It was heavy, and it took all of Tommy to tilt it down off the wall and drag it out of the barn, along the packed earth, and to the barren side of the house below his loft window. All the while, he could hear the creakling of the vine. It was coming from behind the house. From the pasture. And from the cornfield. Even from the other side of the trace far beyond the well and outhouse. Another patch of it was encroaching the grove. Tommy had to hurry.

And he was growing hungry tired. The ladder grew heavier as he weakened in his trudge from the barn to the farmhouse. He was holding one end of the ladder at his waist as he finally leaned his back against the wall of the house and breathed hard. But there was no time to rest. Pawpa needed saving now, so Tommy shrieked again and heaved the ladder up over his head and then started walking it, like Pawpa's obelisk. But this time it was a ladder up the wall of the old house toward his loft window, for the love of Pawpa. For Ma. For everything left of before.

With the last needed heave, his thin arms started to quiver. The ladder was in place. He allowed himself only one breath to recover as he leaned against the wall underneath the ladder stretching up toward his loft. And then, still wobbly and breathing hard through the slackened jaw of fatigue, he started up. It was an old ladder. And there was no one to hold it. "Always have someone hold the ladder," Pa once told him. "Or you'll fall." The way up was wobbly, half because it was an old, unheld ladder, and half because Tommy had all that trembling—not from fear—but from exhaustion. But he knew that kind of trembling before now, so he continued on up. He knew hunger. His hands reached the ladder's top rail and he looked at the open loft window nearly four feet higher up. He'd need to step dangerous-like, gripping the wall as he might and then stand up and grip the sill of the loft window. So he started to stand on the second-to-last rung, which shouldn't ever be stepped on—and he knew it—but he had to go even one higher. He would need to step onto the very top rail and press his hand on the wall and then flap his other forearm onto the windowsill so he might pull himself up and in. He shouldn't do any of that, but Pawpa needed him. And he needed Pawpa!

So he did it, stepping onto the top rail very careful-like and extending himself straightly as best as best could be up along the farmhouse wall despite his legs' wobbling. And he made it. And he

THE CREAKLING

pulled up. His head, upper chest, and arms were in the loft. But he pushed off maybe a bit too hard. As the ladder fell away his eyes widened. He was inside, but he didn't like the sound of the ladder scratching along the side of the house and then hitting the earth.

"But Pawpa," he thought.

He pulled hard, bringing himself all the way through the window before falling weakly into the loft. "I'm here, Pawpa!" he called out. But nothing came back to his ears. "I'll find you!" he added as he lumbered himself up onto the mattress. He was so tired. "Pawpa?"

Still nothing but the creakling in his home came back to him. So he crawled along the mattress with what strength was left in him to the sideboard edge of the loft. He peered over it.

It was a horror below. Barely visible down in the sitting room, Pawpa was entangled in vine. There were several inch-thick and thicker twists of stems all around him. Latched and tightened shoots and sprouts had sunk into him. He couldn't move. The vine was also crawling all up the walls and all along the flooring. So many sprouts. Leaves and shoots were spreading out. Creakling. Thriving. The room was alive and full of the twisted vine several feet deep in places, all stemming from two very thick vines entering from the open bedroom and kitchen windows. Tommy was watching the slow consumption of his home.

Then he heard the voice again.

"Tommy!" Pawpa called out dry-like through the vine. *"I burn, Tommy."*

"I know, Pawpa!" is all Tommy could cry.

"I had to do it, Tommy. Kept it secret."

"I know it, Pawpa. It was just because, Pawpa! I know it. It was just because of Pa!"

There was a sudden gasp as the creakling around Pawpa lurched into new twists and extensions over and into him. Shoots tugging back against his drying flesh.

"Pawpa!" Tommy cried out upon seeing what he could of his grandfather's desiccation below as another series of shoots and

51

sprouts whipped and wrapped and sunk into him and tugged. He was shrinking. Fading. The last of Tommy's family was drying up barely seen before him into a leathery collapse of brittleness. Death. Tommy looked away, then threw himself down on his quilts, pressing his face into them. He cried and screamed and cried again, digging himself into the quilts, holding them so hard, and wetting them with tears.

* * *

Weeping calms a person as it comes to its end, and two minutes later Tommy's body lay relaxed in his loft. His breathing was almost normal apart from sporadic light gasps. His eyes were red and unfocused toward the ceiling. He could hear the creakling. He looked toward the edge of the loft.

Two feet away from him, a one-inch-thick shoot from a vine that had crawled up from below lapped onto the sideboard of the loft. The shoot tightened, pulling up with it a three-inch-thick length of vine. Its leaves were unfolding. Tommy yelped and scurried back, tugging the two quilts with him toward the open loft window. Nothing to tie them onto as a rope down. He'd have to fall from a window fifteen feet up. He looked down to the twelve-foot ladder fallen to the ground. He'd likely land on that, maybe snapping an ankle or worse. That's when Tommy had a dark, dark thought. "How can I escape the vine with a broken leg or hip? It's gonna get me just like Pawpa. *Just like Pawpa!*" And then he made a sound the likes of which he had never made before. It was the damnedest-long howl of a one-word lament: "Mama!"

As his lament came to an end, Tommy heard his own name called back to him from far away. He spun his look out the window, first to the grove. Nothing at the graves. Nothing but the encroaching creakling. Then to the road. Tommy's eyes widened. It was Loretta, running from the trace onto the packed earth alongside the cornfield. "Tommy!" She called again. "Where are you?"

"Up here!" Tommy called, waving an arm out the loft window.

THE CREAKLING

Her expression told that she didn't like the look of the house, and not because it was rather simple and rather worn out like Tommy, but because of the viny growth that spread from the weedy side all into and upon and partly over it. She was looking at it and breathing hard. "Tommy it's crawling all over inside and out!" she said, looking away from the door and nearing the loft-side of the house.

"I know."

"Where's your grandpa?"

"He'd dead, Loretta. That vine done got him. Dried him out."

"O Tommy! What do we do?"

"I told you to go home!"

Loretta looked at the fallen ladder and then up at Tommy. "I was goin'—but Billy-Boy was running to see what was happening. Just truant-like. 'Would get a lickin',' for it, he said. Miss Koehler is probably all-agitated something fierce. But we ran back up to the creek so I could show him all that spreading vine and even the growth further ahead. I sent him back to tell it all. To save the town."

"Were the wheel tracks still clear?"

"Uh-huh," she said, but it's getting' close in so many places. "We should go, Tommy."

"I know it."

"It's all in the house. Can you get down?"

"There's no way without the ladder. And I might break bad if I jumped!"

She looked over it all. And she looked at the old wooden ladder on the parched earth. "Tommy. I'm gonna lift it to you!"

The ladder was give-or-take almost three times her height, and it weighed maybe as much as she did. Tommy watched her pull the ladder away from the house a bit and then align it and then tip it sideways and then try to heft it up. But that try failed. It was heavy. So she went at it again. Tommy coached her something, but she said "I *know* it, Tommy!" She then set about correcting her try perfect-like. In a minute, she was tired and leaning against the wall, but she also had the ladder leaning a few feet up against the wall. Nearly shoulder-height to her.

"I'll walk it up," she said.

The creakling was louder behind him, so he looked back over his shoulder. New sprouts were lapping out onto the edge of the mattress and then gripping it, pulling more vine up as they tightened. More leaves were unfolding. It was taking over the loft, but Tommy kept quiet about all that. He just pulled the quilts a bit closer to him. "Be patient. If you rush, you might fail it all," Pawpa once said. Tommy knew he should listen to Pawpa, so he didn't tell Loretta how close the creakling was. Nothing to do but hope.

Within a minute, the ladder thumped its last, walked thump along the outside wall. A very steep angle. Like before, the top rung was some four feet below the window.

"I'll hold it strong, Tommy," she said, coming around the ladder and straddling it and leaning against it with a strong grip. "I won't let it move."

"Watch out, first," he said.

She looked up.

He was wadding up Ma's quilt. "We're taking these," he said before throwing it well away from her onto the earth below. He then did the same for Mawma's quilt.

He then started his climb out the loft window. Seated upon the windowsill he rolled onto his belly with his legs reaching down. He began lowering himself, looking at the creakling in his home eroding everything slowly away. He lowered himself a bit more, one forearm yet on the sill. He gave another thought to Pawpa. But there was nothing he could do but love him so much.

"That's right, Tommy," Loretta said. "Maybe just one foot lower."

With his chin and clutching hands yet upon the sill, his toes touched the top rail. And the ladder didn't sway. "I'm leaning hard and it ain't movin', Tommy. Just stay straight. Straight down the ladder."

THE CREAKLING

Tommy listened to her. With his torso pressed against the wall, he straightened himself as best he could imagine and then released his grip from the window. His hands pressed against the wall, steadying his slight wobble atop the ladder.

"Slow now, Tommy," Loretta said. "One step straight down. I'll catch you if you fall."

Her saying that was the end of him! So he took that one step straight down. And the rung was there. The ladder barely moved. With his cheek and chest against the wall, he reached down and felt the top of the ladder and took another step down and then another. He was safer now and low enough now. Even if he fell, he probably wouldn't be too hurt.

She stepped away as he neared the bottom of the ladder. She had a little grin. "I held it good, didn't I?"

"Yes, Loretta. You did," he said with a very tired smile on his face. "You did!"

Neither knew what to do at that moment as they looked at each other. He thought about hugging her, but he was full of tired thinking and waited too long. So the creakling in the fields took back their focus.

"We have to leave," Tommy began. "Yes?"

"Right."

"But I don't want any of that vine touching us along the trace." He looked to the barn and then to the creakling in the back pasture. "We have time to hitch up the oxcart. For a better chance."

Loretta looked to the well a second. "Lemme have some water first, Tommy," she began. "I've been so thirsty since lunch."

* * *

They were smiling at each other. Tommy pulled up the bucket and set it on the wall of the well. As she cupped her hands into the water, Tommy looked down. All by itself at the edge of the well was the smallest branch of the purplish vine and a tiny leaf and a shoot whipping around and coiling against a blade of grass. "Don't!"

Tommy called, slapping her hands and spilling the water before it touched her lips. His hard slap was the first time he had touched her.

"Tommy!" she exclaimed before seeing his eyes and looking where he looked. "Oh, Tommy!" she exclaimed differently, taking a step back and looking at the bit of vine, the pail, and then at her wet hands. "Is it in the water?"

But it was a curious thing. Some of the water that was slapped from her hands had fallen on the little growth of vine, and the vine didn't like that. It coiled up on itself, paling and shrinking. The leaf drooped, and the shoot retracted. Was it dying?

"Look at that!" Tommy said.

"But the creek water made it grow."

Tommy took a knee. The vine was still retracting, slowly now, and it was paling. It was coming to a stop. "Maybe it's the sulfur."

"Tommy?"

He looked to Loretta, who was now bowed a bit beside him. "Mawma and Pawpa used powdered sulfur on crops to keep the fungus away—back when we had a better farm. But you mustn't put too much on mustang grape and other vine. Ruins vine plants or the fruit, somehow. But I don't know the why or how."

"Let's try a bucket on a cornfield patch of it and see."

Tommy smiled. "That's smart!" He unfastened the bucket. And they walked up near a spot at the edge of the cornfield where the vine had reached. "Let's not get too close if the splashing breaks pieces off toward us."

"That's smart."

"Ready?"

She nodded.

It was what they hoped for. The twisted, reddish-purple and glossy assemblage of vine and leaf and sprout and shoot that was hit by that sulfury well water recoiled almost immediately. And it made a noise as the well water seeped in. Almost like a backward hiss in its wettened crumpling. It was an undoing.

THE CREAKLING

They looked at each other. Tommy smiled first. And then they hugged real quick. Just for a moment. And almost without even thinking.

"I'm drinkin' some of it, Sulfur Tommy," she said with her nose scrunched the way it was sometimes. "Because your water kills it," she added. "And I'm thirsty, and who knows what the water will be like when we get back into town."

Despite the creakling all around, she was smiling calm-like as he reattached the bucket, dropped it down, and hoisted it back up full of water. And that's when Suck-Tooth and Sulfur Tommy shared some sulfury well water from the bucket, drinking it together from their own cupped hands. And for the first time, maybe, Tommy thought it tasted very good.

* * *

Big Waddle and So-Soda were compliant. Tommy never before yoked and hitched them all on his own, but he knew what to do. Pawpa had him help so many times. Pawpa taught him right. And they weren't the largest oxen by far, so the yoke was light enough for Tommy to handle it all by himself, although he was happy to have Loretta's help as they did all of that upon the parched earth at the hitching post just outside the barn.

"You done that fast," Loretta said after Tommy attached the cart's tongue to the yoke and stood up with an exhale. "I can saddle my horse and I twice steered our four horse team in their harrowing, but I ain't never worked oxen."

Tommy liked hearing all that, even though the creakling was closing in on the barn. He was hungry, but refreshed by the well water. "I ain't never harrowed with horses but once with Pawpa a long time ago." He goaded Big Waddle and So-Soda lightly. "Back. Back, now. Come on *back*." And they did. "Haw, now! *Haw*. That's right. Good Waddle. Good So-So. Good Big Waddle. Good So-Soda." The cart was now lined up straight, ready to head out onto the trace. Tommy smiled as he patted a jowl of each ox. He was lucky.

That was maybe the best he'd ever done alone backing up and lining up the oxen. And he done it in front of Loretta. He then went and hefted into the cart the stubby quarter keg of well water they had filled. "I think we're ready, Loretta," Tommy said. "Except for one thing."

"What's that?"

Tommy took up the two quilts and doubled them over before setting them one on top of the other over the cart seat. "For some comfort," Tommy said.

Loretta liked that, and she reached for the seat and started to put her foot on a wheel rung to pull herself up, but Tommy had quickly taken a knee and interlaced the fingers of his hands to make a step for her. "You're real light, so hop on up, my Little Miss Knapp."

She did, after the shortest, slightest giggle. She then sat upon the cart seat, smiling as she adjusted her dress some. Tommy went around to the other side and, having taken his place on their seat, he took up the reins.

"What did you call me?" Loretta asked.

"I didn't mean nothin' by it, Loretta. You're real light, 'cause you're skinny, but not too skinny like me."

Loretta shook her head just slightly. "Not *that*."

"Get up!" Tommy said with a tap of the goad at Big and So-So. The oxen began moving at their slow pace along the packed earth leading away from the farmstead toward the trace leading toward town. Once out on that trace, Tommy wouldn't even need to steer. The oxen knew by rote every dip and distortion along the way. Back in the day, no one needed to steer them long-gone wagon horses, neither. Animals ain't dumb. They'd walk the line as well as humans. Nothin' wants weeds and huisache scratchin' them nonstop. But that time in the wagon was long gone. And that was all right for Tommy.

"No. I meant the other part." Loretta's voice sounded sweet. "You called me somethin'."

THE CREAKLING

With her sweetness, Tommy knew that he wouldn't have to steel himself anymore against some hope or fear of her. He could tell her anything. Even Pawpa would have said so—and that thought made Tommy sad and happy all at once. He smiled. "Loretta Mae," he began, turning his look to her and talking soft but serious. "You're my Little Miss Knapp and I love you."

She smiled her toothy smile so beautiful and held her look at him a moment before scrunching her nose. "Mister Tomas Jones Calhoun, I do believe you are courtin' me!" She then scooted just a bit closer to him, taking up more of their quilted bench as they headed out onto the trace.

She was like sunshine to Tommy.

Made in the USA
Middletown, DE
24 July 2024